LILI'S PUMPKINS

By Maggie Felsch

Illustrated by Ecaterina Leascenco

<u>Challenge Words</u>

package

soil

leaves

orange

sharing

Chapter 1

Lily and her twin brother, Luke, lived in a lighthouse on Firefly Island.

One day a small package came for them.

"It's from Grandmother!" Lily said.

The twins set the box
on the table and opened
it. Even the kitty wanted
to see what was in it.

Inside the box there
were two small bundles,
one for Luke and one for
Lily.

Luke opened his bundle.

"An arrowhead!" he
cried. "A real arrowhead!"

Lily opened her bundle.

Inside were three little
seeds and a note.

Dear Lily,

I am sending you three pumpkin seeds. Care for them wisely, and they will give you joy.

Love,

Grandmother

Lily smiled. "Oh! I can grow my own pumpkin garden! May I plant the seeds, Mom?"

Dad said, "Let's go find a good garden spot. You may plant the seeds in the morning."

Lily set the three pumpkin seeds on the tabletop and went outside with her dad.

Soon they picked a nice spot by Dad's workshop. Lily felt like it was the perfect spot for her garden.

Chapter 2

As soon as sunlight started filling the sky the next morning, Lily woke with a happy feeling.

She dressed, did her chores without being asked, and made oatmeal for everybody.

After breakfast, Lily took her pumpkin seeds outside to her garden spot.

It was a perfect bright and sunny day to plant the pumpkins.

Lily raked the warm soil with her hands.

"This will be a nice spot to grow pumpkins," she said.

She took the first
pumpkin seed and set it
in the soil.

Then she slid a bit of dirt over the seed and patted it with care.

She planted the second
and third seeds in the
same way, two feet apart.

"Now the seeds need water."

Lily filled her mom's watering can and watered the seeds.

"Okay, little pumpkin seeds," Lily said softly, "now it's up to you to grow."

Chapter 3

For a whole week, Lily went to her garden every morning, but nothing had happened.

She watered the seeds.

She watched, and she waited. Luke watched, too.

On day nine, something happened!

Lily bent close to the soil for a better look.

Two tiny leaves were poking up from all three seeds!

"Luke! Come and see!" Lily called.

Luke came over.

"Good work, Lily!" Luke said when he saw the little green leaves.

Lily felt so happy.

The tiny plants grew fast. Lily never forgot to water them or check on them.

Weeds also started to grow and grow.

Lily spent time almost every day pulling weeds.

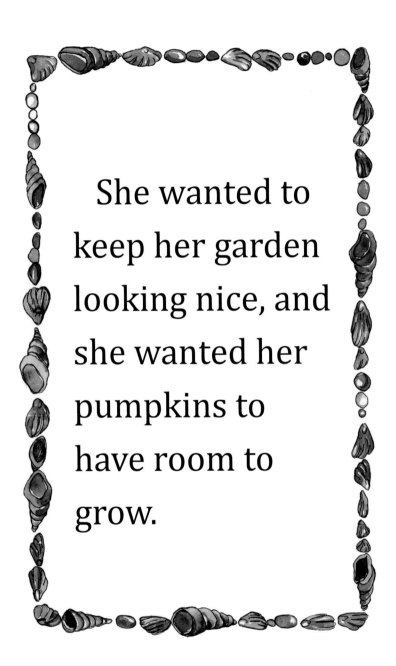

She wanted to keep her garden looking nice, and she wanted her pumpkins to have room to grow.

One day, little green balls started to form on the vines.

"Look! Pumpkins!" Lily told Luke.

"Those?" Luke asked.
"Pumpkins are orange!
And pumpkins are big!"

"These will get big and orange." Lily smiled.
"Wait and see."

Chapter 4

The pumpkins did grow bigger and bigger. One pumpkin was spotted with orange.

Soon it was orange all over and so big!

As Lily was in her garden looking at her big, orange pumpkin, her mom came over.

"A new family lives in
the yellow home at
Crabapple Beach," Mom
told Lily.

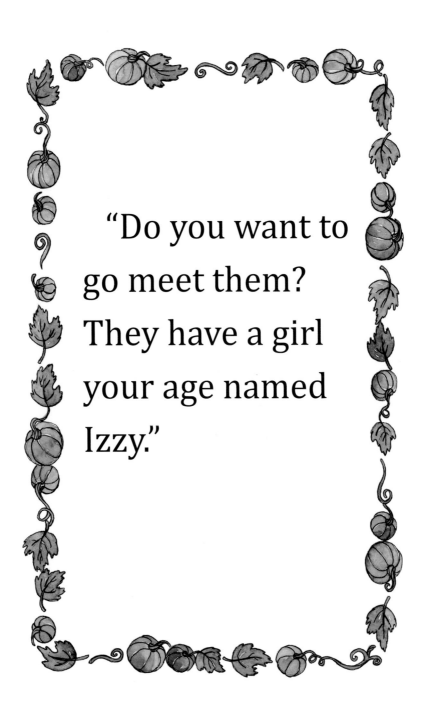

"Do you want to go meet them? They have a girl your age named Izzy."

"Oh, yes!" Lily said.

"Mom, can I give my big,
orange pumpkin to Izzy?"

"Do you want to?" Mom asked. "You only have one big, orange pumpkin."

"I do want to!" Lily said.
"I will have more soon,
and sharing gives me joy."

So Lily, Luke, Mom, and
Dad walked together to
the yellow home at
Crabapple Beach.

Lily gave Izzy the big, orange pumpkin.

"Thank you so much!" Izzy said. "I love it!"

Luke, Lily, and Izzy played leapfrog and beanbag toss until it was time for the twins to go home.

It was a cold walk back to the lighthouse, but Lily felt warm in her heart.

She was glad she gave her first big, orange pumpkin to Izzy.

Chapter 5

That night it got colder and colder. Frost grew on the windowpanes.

Luke and Lily pulled the blankets close to stay warm.

In the morning, the whole island was white with frost.

Dad started a fire in the fireplace. Mom put a teapot on the stove.

Luke and Lily got dressed in boots and coats and went out to the garden.

"Oh no," Lily said.

"Lily, I am so sorry," Luke said as he put his arm around his twin.

The frost had killed all the pumpkin plants.

"There will be no more pumpkins," Lily said sadly.

"Are you okay?" Luke asked his sister kindly.

Lily felt a lump in her throat, but she nodded her head.

"Do you wish you had
kept your big, orange
pumpkin?" Luke asked.

Lily looked at her
brother for a moment.
Then she smiled.

"No, Luke," she said at last. "I am sad that the pumpkins froze, but I am happy that I shared."

The rest of the day,
Luke was extra kind to
his sister.

Chapter 6

A week after the cold night, Izzy and her mom walked to the lighthouse.

Izzy was holding a great big pumpkin pie in her arms.

"My mom helped me bake this pie," Izzy told Luke and Lily.

"I want to share it with you. Sharing makes me happy."

"Thank you, Izzy," Luke
and Lily said, and they all
went inside the
lighthouse.

The pie was so yummy!
Luke and Lily both had
seconds.

"Will you show me how
to make pumpkin pie?"
Lily asked Izzy.

"My mom and I will
show you how!" Izzy told
her.

Then Lily looked out the window at her garden.

"Oh. I forgot. There are no more pumpkins."

Luke told Izzy and her mom what the cold night did to Lily's garden.

Izzy held a little bag out to Lily.

"Open it," Izzy said.

Lily opened the bag. Inside were so many pumpkin seeds!

"They are from the big, orange pumpkin you gave me," Izzy said.

"I can grow lots more
pumpkins!" Lily smiled.

"I am so glad I shared
the big, orange pumpkin."